AF440012

The Girl in the Well

A Story of Courage and Perseverance

By Siddharth Sen

In Memory of my Loving Father

First they ignore you, then they laugh at

you, then they fight you, then you win!

~Mahatma Gandhi

Preface

Story of Rani is inspired by some real-life events. This interesting mystery thriller is based on the ordinary people who become extraordinary when situation demands.

As we turn the pages of this tale, we witness Rani's unwavering courage to battle through the mysteries behind her abduction and uncover the truth. Her story stands as a testament to the formidable strength found within resilience, determination, and the relentless pursuit of truth.

So, dear readers, join me as we embark on this treacherous journey, where hope battles against darkness, where justice triumphs over corruption, and where the indomitable spirit shines through, inspiring us all to fight for what is right and to never falter in the face of adversity.

Siddharth Sen

Disclaimer

All characters, names, places, and events mentioned in this story are fictional and have no relation to anyone or anything real or dead.

It's my creative work, and all references used here are my perspective in the story with no intention to hurt any sentiments of any profession, gender, creed, religion, or caste.

Acknowledgments

Thanks to my family whose support helped me in developing the character and the story concept. The inspiration behind the story is several needy people who are misguided by a corrupt society to commit a crime.

So with heartfelt gratitude, thank you for your love and support and this novel is dedicated to all those families who know the power of perseverance and fight till the end with righteous means.

Rebirth

Sometimes, when we are weakest,

we find the strength to become the strongest

and embark on journeys

we never could have anticipated.

A newfound hope and courage

take hold of us,

and we start afresh, as if reborn!

~ ~ ~ ~ ~ ~ ~

1 : Was it a Dream?

~~~~~~~~~~~~

Scene 1

~~~~~~~~~~~~

"It's so dark here. Is anyone there? Hello, can anybody hear me?" I have no idea where I am.

I find myself sitting in a dimly lit room, lying on what seems to be a bed, although I am not entirely sure. I have just opened my eyes and have no clue, what has happened to me. Feeling tired with a throbbing headache, I close my eyes once again.

~~~~~~~~~~~~

Scene 2

~~~~~~~~~~~~

At another location, a security guard observes four monitors in front of him. One shows a lady on a ventilator, another captures Rani sleeping in the dimly lit room, and the other two show two girls sleeping in separate dark rooms.

A portly man with a French beard enters and asks the guard, "How are they doing?"

"All fine!" the guard replies.

"Keep them ready for tomorrow!" the portly man instructs before leaving.

~ ~ ~ ~ ~ ~ ~ ~ ~ ~ ~

Scene 3

~ ~ ~ ~ ~ ~ ~ ~ ~ ~ ~

Suddenly, there is commotion all around me. I feel jostled, my eyes hurt. However, when I open my eyes, I realize I am on a bustling street. Was it all just a bad dream?

A young boy sits beside me, playing a mouth organ. I feel lost and confused. What is happening? Where am I?

"What is this place?" I ask the boy, but he does not look at me.

I wave my hand in front of him, causing him to stop playing and look at me.

He has beautiful turquoise eyes, and gazing into them brings me a profound sense of relaxation, causing me to forget my question.

"You were asking something?" the boy asks.

Feeling anxious, I respond, "Yes, do you know how long I've been here with you?"

I tap my head, realizing that this is not my original question.

"I am not sure; you were already here when I arrived this morning. You have been sleeping since then as if you were exhausted. Did you sleep here all night?" the boy stares at me intently.

"I don't know; I am unsure what happened to me. What is this place?"

"You are in Chinatown, and this is the marketplace," he replies sweetly. However, I cannot comprehend how I ended up in Chinatown. What is going on?

I thank him, and he resumes playing his mouth organ. Passers-by drop coins and money for him. I remember now the tune he is playing; it is one of my favourites from the movie Sholay. Is he truly a talented beggar, or is there more to him?

I search through my jacket pockets and find some money and a crumpled newspaper.

The old newspaper bears a date of October eighth. Seeing this, I have a flashback. I recall tearing this piece from the Sunday Times before a job interview. I remember waiting in line for an interview and drinking the orange juice served to all six candidates. After that, everything becomes a blur.

I immediately ask the boy for the current date.

He replies, "It's December thirty-first!"

~ ~ ~ ~ ~ ~ ~ ~ ~ ~ ~ ~ ~

Rani realizes that something has happened to her in the past three months. But how will she find out what transpired? Is it worth taking the risk? As a reporter, she knows she must find out. After all, who knows what else is happening in this town?

Rani, originally from Guwahati, moved to Kolkata a few months ago after a fight with her family regarding her marriage. She had been desperately searching for jobs before she got kidnapped!

2 : Destroyed

Siraj was in a tense mood when Adhikari entered the room.

"Did you hear the news?" Adhikari asked.

"Yes, and I am unsure how we will handle this escalation. Even you are not responding to my calls! My head was exploding with all kinds of thoughts! What happened to you? Why weren't you picking up my calls?" Siraj complained to Adhikari.

"I didn't because anyone can track these calls; throw away that SIM card and get a new one; I don't want any more troubles. I just had a conversation with my boss, and he also asked to close all the hotels in the town and move the girls to some different place. We will have to go underground, pack your things, and we need to leave immediately, right now!"

"But what will happen to Magan? He got already arrested by the police." Siraj looked nervous, as Magan was the man linked to the kidnappings, and if he confessed, then all get convicted.

"You don't have to worry; Boss will take care of him; let's just get out of here and burn whatever we have here. I know Magan was close to you, but this is not the time to get emotional; he has done his duty and will get his prize!" Adhikari opened the cupboard and filled a bag with all the money and important papers.

Siraj and Magan were very close, as they were from the same village and had spent a good amount of adulthood together working for the then MLA Rajendra Choudhary of Birbhum. When the MLA got murdered by his enemies, they had to run far away from that place to save themselves from the wrath of the locals. They both ran together to Asansol to hide from the immediate threat and during this period, they got close and became good friends. In a few months, their bonding was much stronger than earlier, and they became close friends. It was at this time when they were doing odd jobs like petty thefts and extortions to survive, that they met Adhikari. Now that thinking about losing Magan after eighteen years of friendship made him emotional, he was worried about his life too. But this path of crime had one thing guaranteed, an untimely death. Though he was not afraid to die earlier, now he was, as he had fallen in love with a nurse Bhavna who gave them medical supplies.

Adhikari was a dreaded criminal and ruthless to the core; for him, only two things mattered: his share of money and his son Gagandeep. His share kept him loyal to the boss, and

Gagandeep's needs kept him motivated to earn more and more money.

Adhikari had three wives, and none of them had children. That is when he married for the fourth time to a Sikh girl, Karandeep. This girl he had kidnapped once and later fell in love with couldn't resist another namesake marriage. Karandeep's parents were dead, and she was taken care of by her uncle, who used to abuse her every day, and even by her uncles' friends. So when she got kidnapped, she didn't resist but was happy to get rid of that rotten family. When she gave birth to a son, Adhikari became possessive about her and his son, Gagandeep, but after six years, Karandeep died of pneumonia, and Gagandeep, was admitted into a boarding school. Adhikari wanted Gagandeep to get a good education and settle in some important post, away from this criminal life.

Siraj had never met the boss but only heard his voice, so for him, Adhikari's message meant the boss's message, and he agreed with him to get ready and quickly left the office after burning all their details available in that office.

However, their destiny had some other plans. Little did they know, despite their efforts to eliminate any trace of their activities, they would soon find themselves caught red-handed!!

3 : A Wanted

It was one o'clock; the recess was getting over, but Shantanu was not happy.

Typically, after eating the sumptuous delicacies his wife cooked and packed for him, he got elated and used to get boosted up for his after-break classes. But today, even though Meena, his wife, had prepared his favourite jackfruit curry and the tomato chutney to savour, he still felt uneasy.

No, it was not the food, but what he had seen in the last period of seventh grade. The class was very naughty in general, and he used to enjoy teaching them, but one of the students was unusual today.

There was an intelligent boy who was mischievous too; most of the days planned pranks with his classmates and then used to extend some of them to teachers as well, like drawing their caricature on the blackboard or sticking chewing gum on the teacher's chair, and many more. The class enjoyed these fun acts, and being a boys boarding school away from their homes, they found peace in these activities.

Though the other teachers were annoyed with this rowdy class, and most of the time whole class was either standing on their respective chairs as a punishment or making rounds of the playground, Shantanu was never annoyed with them.

Shantanu considered this was a period when they started understanding the various shades of life around them, so being mischievous was normal. He used to give directions to channel this energy into creative tasks to enhance their imaginations. Since he was a mathematics teacher, he used to task them with fun problems, and leverage indoor and outdoor movements, to strengthen their analytical skills. While the children loved his methods, he was not a favourite of his peers or the headmaster because of his ways of teaching.

Coming to this morning's experience, when he went to class seven and was expecting some mischief as usual, he was surprised to find the class very quiet, and the most silent was Gagandeep.

The intelligent prankster was looking sad, and the class was too. Though he thought of asking what happened, he had to finish a few critical lesson points, and somehow he couldn't check out the problem. He was thinking about catching up with Gagandeep after the class got over, but then the next lesson teacher entered.

Gagandeep was the son of a wealthy businessman. Since his mother passed away while he was very young and his father was mostly away due to work, he never got family love. His father used to visit him on every vacation but never took him to his home. They went sightseeing, stayed in resorts, and always spent his vacation days camping or roaming around new places. Initially, he liked these trips, but then he got satiated with them and longed for home. He doubted that his father had some affair that he was trying to hide.

He was getting paranoid about his father's relationship, and one day he asked him directly, Papa, why don't we go home anytime? What are you trying to hide from me?"

"Nothing like that, Son! Why would I hide anything from you? Nothing is in that vacant house after your mother left me, so why waste your vacation in that dark place?"

When he got this answer from his father, his eyes were as cold as a stone; something like a suspicion was now rooted deeper. He started creating the notion that maybe his father only killed his mother, but it was not easy to find out, so he acted normal, and years passed like this. At school, he kept these emotions at bay and enjoyed being busy with mischief and games.

But a message from an unknown number in the morning suddenly changed his mood!

It said, 'Your father is a wanted criminal.'

Who sent this message, and why was his father a Wanted Criminal unsettled little Gagandeep?

4 : A Breaking News

Everywhere in the city, it was the same breaking news. A leopard had attacked a hostel and killed five kids, and now is running away with one kid. This news was creating havoc in the urban communities. If a leopard can attack a well-guarded hostel in the middle of the city, the flats and independent houses are in great danger.

A CCTV clip on all the major channels displayed how the large leopard carried a kid's body. How can this happen? Where are the cops? And how did this leopard enter the city? The leopard was at least seven feet long and appeared to be more than eighty kilos; this was the heaviest leopard anybody had seen. The reporters were questioning law enforcement and forest officials about the origin of the large carnivore, but unfortunately, nobody had any answers. Everyone was afraid and didn't know how to deal with the situation. Was it a man-

eater, or by mistake, it attacked humans?

Well, in our country, people start connecting these types of events with religious sentiments too, as some High priests appeared on one of the news channels, stating that it's not a leopard but an incarnation of Goddess Kali, angry at people for their disrespect of religion, immediately there is a need to do a grand ritual to make her happy and forgive the people of this place.

While the police and forest officials had no clue how to catch the leopard, now based on religious sentiments, people started believing the Priest's story of its connections with a Goddess. This belief suddenly started yielding huge donations for a big ritual ceremony. All of this was causing enough confusion in Shantanu's life.

Shantanu had planned to talk to his student Gagandeep in the morning about his unusual behaviour but didn't get a chance, and then by the evening, this leopard news had turned the city into chaos. Everybody was rushing home and trying to safeguard themselves. The government declared a holiday for all schools, markets, and offices and planning to impose an emergency curfew to handle the situation. The administration had no clue where the leopard went and who was his next prey.

Shantanu was a local of the city and stayed a little far from the boarding school where he taught mathematics. His wife, Meena, was worried when she heard about the leopard attack event. Later was happy to discover that the hostel was not her husband's school.

Now she wanted Shantanu to be home until the leopard scare got resolved. Shantanu was getting restless about the state of the city. If the government imposed a curfew, it would be very unplanned. He had to get some groceries stocked before it was too late.

"I have to get some groceries, Meena; otherwise, if there is a curfew, it will be hard to survive! Let me go out; the leopard has attacked the other side of the city, and I assure you, I will be back before he catches me!" Shantanu somehow convinced Meena in his humorous way and left for the grocery store.

The sight on the street was devastating. Everyone was in a hurry, some running, some speeding, all trying to get home at the earliest.

He quickly walked past the street corner towards the nearby grocery store and observed that the fear of life was turning people inhumane too. A young adult on a bike crushed a street dog and sped. It was a selfish society. His eyes were sad looking at this scene, but he was in a hurry too! Then suddenly he saw a young boy unexpectedly running towards the dog out of nowhere!

There was too much crowd, and Shantanu couldn't resist; he ran towards the boy, guarded him, and took shelter near the pavement.

"What were you doing running in the middle of the road if a car or bike ran over you? Where are your parents?" Shantanu enquired.

"I am an orphan!"

Shantanu thought for a second and immediately decided to save this boy and maybe adopt him too. Shantanu and Meena had no kids, even after ten years of marriage.

A disaster event day became a miracle moment for Shantanu!

But was this orphan boy, really an orphan?

5 : A Story of Injustice

In a small village near Dhaka, Bangladesh, Ali lived happily with his mother, wife, and eight-year-old daughter, Muskaan. His fruit business was thriving, and he had managed to repair his shop earlier this year before the rains. This improvement had increased his sales since customers could now buy fruits without getting drenched during downpours, unlike the other shops that lacked a shed. Another reason for his success was his competitive pricing and high-quality fruits, which earned him loyal and satisfied customers.

Ali's wife, Nikhat, was a diligent and attractive person who always wore a smile on her face. Her family meant everything to her. She worked tirelessly day and night, managing the household chores, her daughter's studies, and attending to her mother-in-law's needs. Additionally, she assisted Ali in his business by handling his accounts and communicating with suppliers, ensuring they consistently obtained competitive prices. Nikhat also possessed excellent bargaining skills.

Thanks to Nikhat's hard work and intelligence, Ali's business was booming, and he was free from debt. However, his success stirred jealousy among his neighbours, particularly Kader, who owned a fruit shop nearby and was losing customers to Ali.

One busy day, after finishing her cooking, Nikhat was about to bathe when someone knocked on the door. Her mother-in-law, who slept near the door, abruptly woke up upon hearing the knock.

"Who is it?" she inquired in her usual hoarse voice.

"It's the postman. There's a letter for Nikhat Begum," the outsider shouted.

The mother called for Nikhat to retrieve the letter. Nikhat, who had already undressed in preparation for her shower, heard her mother's voice and hastily wrapped a saree around herself before opening the door.

~~~~~~~~~~~

Later in the afternoon, when Ali returned home for lunch, he was horrified by the scene that unfolded before him.

The door was left ajar, and his mother lay on the floor, her white saree stained with blood, her throat slit, and the room drenched in a pool of blood. Ali frantically called for Nikhat, but she was nowhere to be found. He was devastated. Hearing his shouts and screams, Fahad, Ali's childhood friend, and neighbour, rushed to see what had happened.

Fahad was shocked by the brutal scene before him. He tried to pull Ali out of the house, but Ali felt lost in that moment.
~~~~~~~~~~~

Recognizing it as a crime scene, Fahad promptly called the police station and informed them of the situation.

"Ali, what happened here?" the inspector asked.

Ali was in a state of shock and unable to speak. The police began searching the house, which was in disarray. The kitchen utensils were scattered on the floor, indicating a struggle that had taken place throughout the house. In one corner, there lay a wet saree stained with blood.

Meanwhile, Ali's daughter returned from school and met a large crowd and the presence of police officers, which both intrigued and frightened her. Muskaan tried to push her way through the crowd to enter her house when a lady constable stopped her and prevented her from entering.

"This is my home. What happened? Mom and Dad? Where are you?" Muskaan shouted.

Upon hearing Muskaan's voice, Ali snapped out of his daze as if life in him was back.

"Muskaan, I'm here. Come here, my dear!" Ali's eyes welled up with tears as he saw Muskaan.

Ali and Fahad stood outside the house, observing the police conduct their investigation. However, Ali had not spoken a word to anyone until that moment. Hearing Ali speak and realizing he had a daughter, the inspector took them aside.

"Did you come from school?" the inspector asked Muskaan.

"Yes, where is Mom? Where is Grandma? Papa, please tell me what happened." Muskaan remained oblivious to the situation.

Ali looked at her, and suddenly, the realization struck him that Nikhat was missing! He fell to his knees, pleading with the inspector to find his wife.

"Please, Inspector Sir, please find my wife!"

The inspector gave him a stern look and instructed his constables to handcuff him and Fahad, taking them both to the police station.

Later in the station, Ali got tortured until he falsely confessed to killing his mother and concealing his wife's body. They released Fahad after obtaining Ali's forced confession. The inspector had already received his share from Kader.

Kader had enlisted the help of local thugs to destroy Ali's happy family, rape and murder his wife Nikhat, and ruin his business forever.

Ali's only mistake was his success and happiness in a neighbourhood where everyone else struggled to make a living.

Subsequently, Muskaan was sent to an orphanage, having lost her loving family. Suddenly this society had become inhumane for her, and she didn't want to live there.

Determined to reclaim what was rightfully hers and seek justice, Muskaan pondered how to achieve this. She knew that, to make an impact, she had to become powerful herself, but how?

6 : Somewhere Lost

~~~~~~~~

A local proverb says that when thirsty, we should walk

toward the well; the well will never walk toward us!

~~~~~~~~

Rani's journey had just begun. She found herself on a bustling

road in Chinatown, unconscious with no recollection of the

past three months. Watching herself on the last day before

New Year, stranded in such an unknown place, seemed

disturbing.

The otherwise dingy Chinatown, adorned with splendid

decorations, looked enchanting, celebrating New Year's Eve.

Everywhere she looked, she saw cheerful faces. But what had

transpired during the past three months? Why couldn't she remember anything? Her last memory was visiting a journal office for a job interview as an editor. However, after the polite receptionist handed her a glass of orange juice, her memory went blank. Generally, she would refrain from drinking juice from unknown sources, but that day, nerves and thirst might have gotten the better of her.

Determined to uncover the truth, Rani decided to visit the journal office. Yet, she realized it might be risky to venture alone. She needed to find a companion first.

Years ago, her school friend from Guwahati, Anik, had relocated to Kolkata with his family. Anik, now a police officer, was also her Facebook friend. Though they didn't communicate frequently, considering the circumstances and her unfamiliarity with Kolkata, reconnecting with him seemed like the wisest choice.

Anik's family had settled comfortably in the Salt Lake area of Kolkata. His father, Sunil Bhattacharya, was an IPS officer renowned for his impressive personality, while his mother was a loving homemaker who cared for their three children. Anik had an elder brother Som, who practiced law in the Kolkata High Court, and a younger sister Leena, who was still pursuing her education. Rani had visited their government bungalow in Guwahati numerous times during their childhood. Although their contact had waned since then, she remained friends with Anik on Facebook, and Leena was also part of her friend list.

Rani contemplated meeting Anik informally and confiding in him about her predicament. Thus, she messaged him, informing him of her presence in the city.

Anik had always harboured aspirations of becoming an IPS officer like his father but had eventually settled for the position of sub-inspector. He hadn't cleared the civil service examination yet excelled in the State Service exams, earning a commendable rank. Anik was an intelligent and handsome young man with aspirations of becoming an inspector soon. His colleagues admired his approach to work. While people knew about his influential connections due to his father, he refrained from exploiting them. Anik had maintained his honesty throughout his career and was considered a helpful cop.

Since childhood, Anik had regarded Rani as a dear friend. Their relationship was unlike his other romantic endeavours. Though he had dated several girls, he never allowed their relationship to transcend the boundaries of friendship with Rani. Recognizing her serious nature, he didn't want to jeopardize their pure bond with insincere romantic behaviour. Thus, he remained connected to her as a true friend and guide. Rani even supported him during the distress period. Anik had broken after failing to clear the civil service exam. Rani continuously encouraged him to prepare for state service exams.

Rani found herself far away from home, abandoned by her parents due to her elopement from a prearranged marriage. In this unfamiliar city, she felt like an outsider. Her only hope was to find a companion in Anik who could assist her in uncovering the secrets and understanding what had befallen her over the past three months!

Consequently, when Rani abruptly messaged Anik about being in the city, he felt delighted and eager to meet her and responded to her immediately.

7 : The Meeting

In a white shirt, black trousers, and grey sunglasses, Anik appeared hero-like as he entered the coffee shop. Rani was already there, waiting for him. Unlike girls who make boys wait, she wasn't here to throw tantrums. Rani despised those who didn't respect time. She was always punctual and expected the same from others. Today she arrived earlier than the agreed time because she had a lot to discuss and didn't know how to start.

Anik had no uneasiness in mind; he was thrilled to meet Rani after ten years. Finally, they were meeting face-to-face, and it was an incredible feeling. Although they had stayed connected through calls and sometimes Facebook, meeting in person with Rani was an experience Anik invariably looked forward to.

As Anik entered the coffee shop, he couldn't easily spot Rani, or perhaps she looked different now than in her profile photo. His eyes scanned the crowded place, searching for Rani among the twenty people sitting there.

This place was, crowded as always, and Anik had chosen it because it was popular and his favourite. He had requested Rani to meet there. He knew Rani wasn't a coffee person but wanted to impress her with a tasty coffee.

When Rani noticed Anik struggling to find her, she waved, and their eyes met. Anik felt a bit embarrassed. As a close friend, he should have recognized her on his own. However, he immediately smiled and opened his arms to give Rani a warm hug. Also, releasing his tension of being unable to recognise her in the first place and initiated the conversation on a happy note.

Rani had a beautiful smile, and that priceless moment was enough for Anik to reminisce about their friendship and forget everything else.

"How are you?" they both questioned each other simultaneously and then grinned. Anik held Rani's hands and said, "I'm so happy you're finally here. After ten long years, a lot has changed, but our friendship hasn't. Isn't it marvellous?"

Rani nodded, feeling more at ease. She wasn't sure how Anik would react to her appearance. She had lost weight and had short hair, wearing loose jeans and an oversized black shirt to hide her skinny body. But Anik's words got her confidence back, assuring her that this was the same old Anik.

"I'm a police officer now, thanks to you, Rani. If you hadn't encouraged me, I might have given up, but I'm in my dream job," Anik beamed with pride.

"Yes, you did it, and I'm very happy for you, Anik. It's been a long time, and I wanted to meet you in person to congratulate you, but it didn't happen until now. Finally, we meet, and it's an amazing feeling!" Rani expressed her joy.

"So, how are you? Why did you choose this place? What's been going on? I know I'm asking many questions, but before you answer any of them, let's order something. It is my favourite place, and let me tell the owner to make something special for us! Are you okay with that?" Anik asked excitedly.

"Yes, that's fine, Anik, but I didn't realize this place was so crowded. Is it possible for us to go somewhere else? I have a lot to tell you, and I don't think this is a suitable place for that!" Rani surprised Anik.

"Absolutely! That's fine; we can go to the nearby park. But let me treat you to the special coffee from this place first, and then we can leave. Is that okay?" Anik tried to persuade Rani.

Rani nodded, and Anik placed his coffee order with the familiar waiter for a special cappuccino, who was already overwhelmed to see Anik with another new girl this week!

8 : Spider and Love

While sitting in the crowded place, Rani felt shy about telling her story, but she still loved Anik's company.

An old coffee shop with the strong smell of coffee and freshly baked cookies all over the place was very romantic, even though it was buzzing with people. No one was watching anyone else, as the young couples were busy spending time in each other's company. The place was quite colourful in terms of fashion, too. The nearby college and school kids were its loyal customers, and it was a happy hour too. During happy hour the place had discounts and freebies like garlic bread and finger chips.

"All the crowd here is very young; don't you think we should go somewhere else?" Rani asked Anik.

"Okay, okay, don't worry, we will go now. I just wanted you to get used to city life; it's always busy wherever we go, unlike your quiet home! Let's Go now!" Anik smiled and asked the waiter to add the bill to his account while grabbing Rani's hand and exiting the coffee shop.

Rani was fine about Anik touching her as she treated him like a good friend.

Anik, in his grey sunglasses, was looking handsome; he was still holding her hand while crossing the street and making sure she didn't get lost on the busy road. Then he started walking towards the north and released her hand, letting her follow him through the narrow pavement.

Rani was quiet all this time; she just followed Anik through the busy pavement, which was lively and full of roadside hawker shops selling bangles, clothes, handicrafts, make-up, etc.

A few of the bangle Hawkers tried to persuade Rani to buy the colourful handcrafted bangles, but she ignored them and moved ahead, keeping pace with Anik.

After walking for ten to fifteen minutes, Anik finally stopped and looked back. Rani understood they had reached the point where they could finally sit down and talk in private.

But it was a crowded park again, and she could see a lot of couples there too. She stared at Anik; he smiled and said, with an intended pun, "This is the most private place in the city!"

Anik used his Policeman style to empty a bench from a kissing couple and ask Rani to sit. It was a little awkward for Rani when the couple looked at her with bitterness for a while before moving on.

"Tell me now, what do you want to talk about but couldn't in that coffee shop?" Anik asked Rani quite bluntly.

Yes, finally, Rani felt she could talk about her story now.

"First of all, I am extremely excited that you have not changed even a little bit, Anik! The way you made me cross the road and then took care of me all this while, it's the same old Anik who was my friend from school and always treated me well. I was a little worried in the morning before meeting you, wondering if you had changed. Or how Sub Inspector Anik would treat me? But now I am not feeling worried at all." Rani said with a smile.

Anik smiled. His cheeks turned slightly rosy in response to the unexpected praise. His behaviour around her was typically friendly, so there wasn't anything particularly remarkable about it. However, he also acknowledged Rani's perspective, understanding that this meeting held a special significance. After all, it had been ten years since they last saw each other in person.

Throughout the years, Anik had many female friends, but Rani held a unique place in his heart; she was his best friend.

"I am new to this city, and it looks like it is already hostile!"

Rani spoke about her experience of appearing for the editor's interview and suddenly fainting. Then, waking up in the busy streets of Chinatown after three months was a big mystery for her.

"What should I do now? I couldn't think of anyone else other than you to get help from!" Rani concluded and looked at Anik.

Anik's mind exploded; he was surprised to hear her story and unable to process this information with the speed Rani had told him. He was still thinking.

In the meantime, Rani saw a black spider on Anik's shoulder, and before he could say anything, on impulse, she tried to throw away the spider but slipped, and her hand slapped his face.

"Oh, I am extremely sorry. Very sorry. It was a big spider. I am sorry. Oh no!" Rani was blabbering in shock after slapping Anik.

The slap had surprised Anik too, but then he laughed, observing Rani; her cheeks were far redder than his, which she had slapped hard.

He held Rani's face in both hands and kissed her forehead. "Don't bother, dear; you just saved me from a dangerous spider? Isn't it!!"

Then they both looked at each other and started laughing.

It was pure love of friendship!

Survival

Survival is not for the weakest

but the ones who accept failures

and then fight again

to become Winners!

~ ~ ~ ~ ~ ~ ~

1 : The Sting

Rani was now sure that Anik would help her find the culprits; hence, she decided to go with him to that journal office first.

~~~~~~~~

Anik was on his Royal Enfield today; he picked me up from my women's hostel, and before he could move any further, we got stuck in a wedding crowd.

The groom was on his horse, feeling amused seeing the dance of his relatives when one of the relatives started a snake dance on the road. It is a famous dance in the Northern states of India, but I was seeing it for the first time. The crowd was full of energy and was hooting for that person who appeared crazy with his hands raised and joined like an imitation of a snake head and his whole body moving on the
~~~~~~~~

ground like a snake body grooving to the Nagin (Female Snake) song, while he was making hisses like a real snake.

Anik got down and looked for the traffic police, who were also enjoying the dance, and gave them a good scolding. Then the wedding crowd dispersed within five minutes, clearing the way for Anik and the honking traffic behind us.

He was speeding now, and I was enjoying the power he wielded. While riding with him, my mind was still unable to forget the funny moves of the snake dancer, and I started smiling at the snake hiss he was enacting. Anik could see me in his rear mirror and inquired, "What happened? Why are you smiling? Any jokes?"

"Nothing; I was just thinking about that snake dancer—how crazy people can be!"

"Yes, here people can do anything; they have no fear of the law, and nobody complains too till someone raises their voice; see, even our traffic policemen were getting amused; so think about my situation of dealing with criminals; no one is ready to become a witness easily; only fear of our stick makes them speak!" Anik smirked.

I realized that, as a policeman, Anik's sense of humor had evolved. I agreed with his observation about people's carelessness and lack of empathy, but I pondered silently.

In another few minutes, we were near the journal office. Anik said he would go and check inside and asked me to wait, but I was adamant to go with him as I remembered a few faces and maybe would identify if they were still there. He agreed with one condition: I would not react or speak while he talked, and I nodded.

The journal office was on the fifth floor of an eight-storey building and had no lift.

Anik was athletic, so he quickly walked through the stairs, and I was trying to catch up with him, but by the time I reached the fifth floor, I was gasping for breath. Anik asked me to stay quiet; in my condition, I couldn't talk anyway. He went towards the centre of the large hall on the fifth floor; it had a reception counter, and a receptionist was standing.

"Wait!! It is not the place at all." It struck me that the place looked very different; it was like a pathology centre rather than a journal office, and the receptionist was a new person.

I tried to stop Anik but then thought of staying quiet as he had instructed, so I sat on one of the benches and started observing the place.

Something was odd here; there was a board of the Report Section hanging at the place where earlier it was written, Editor Room when I had come last time.

A person was sitting near the report section who looked familiar, had a beard, and had a scar on his left cheek.

Yes, I remembered him; he had served me poisonous orange juice. Instead of reacting, I slowly took out my phone and, without his notice, took a photo, then realised Anik was walking towards me.

"This is a pathology centre from the last ten years; are you sure you came here for the interview?" Anik asked me.

"Yes, Anik, I am sure I have come here, and this place looked like a journal office then. Believe me and sit near me; I will tell you something." I took his hand and made him sit next to me, and then I showed him the photo of the man behind me getting unconscious last time.

Anik said, "Okay, okay, I believe you; don't do anything now and go down without his notice. I will inquire and get all his background, but you move and wait for me outside this place until this sting operation is over!"

I nodded to his instructions and went down those long stairs again, but I felt very concerned about Anik. Was this normal, or was I falling in love?

2 : The Scar

It was more than half an hour, I was, waiting for Anik in the parking lot. He was not even picking up my call. Suddenly a scary thought crossed my mind, what if Anik also is kidnapped like I was last time?

No, he is a policeman; he should be able to handle them, but then what if they overpower him? My thoughts were killing me when I heard my name.

"Rani, let's get out of here; I think I have some clues!" Anik said.

Thank God Anik was fine. I nodded and sat on his Royal Enfield. Anik drove towards my hostel and dropped me off.

"I will call you at night; I have some urgent work to take care of!" He said that and left.

I was not sure what had happened inside; he didn't even tell me what he learned. It was getting very suspenseful.

I reached my room and went for a shower. It was hot and tiring, so the hot shower was a must to calm my mind.

While having a shower, suddenly I felt something and realised I had an uneven surface near my left side rib, as if there had been some eruption. Strangely, I hadn't noticed this earlier due to my inattentiveness.

The mirror in the bathroom was only up to my face, so I had to use my mobile camera, and then I found I had a stitch-like scar near my left rib. What was this mark?

I dressed up and thought about talking to my hostel mate, Bhavna, a nurse.

I knocked on her door to see if she had returned from work, but there was no answer; she was not back yet.

I thought of calling her number but then decided to wait till she returned and messaged her to call me when she was home. She immediately messaged back, responding yes.

I turned on my favourite music station, and while waiting for her, I remembered all the events from the last two days.

My meeting with Anik in the coffee shop, telling him about the past incidents and my memory loss, then the changed journal office and the bearded peon, Anik was also not telling me anything; what was he hiding from me?

My phone rang while I was getting these thoughts—it was Bhavna!

"I am back and very hungry; come to my room; we will have dinner together!"

Bhavna had gotten two packets of vegetable thali from her canteen; this was our favourite food. I am staying in her friend's room until I find some place for myself as her friend is on vacation.

When I met Bhavna four days ago near the bus stop, I didn't know she would become such a good friend.

I was looking lost, asking for the bus from Chinatown to Naktala, when she found me at the Bus stop. I had a room in Naktala earlier, three months ago, but now I have shifted to her hostel as my old owner has already thrown away my luggage and rented it to a new person since I didn't show up for the last three months.

Well, coming to the present, I was sitting with her to talk about the scar and determined that once we complete dinner, I would discuss with her about this.

"You have been very kind to me, and I like your warm nature!

I need your help on something today; it's about a mark that

I don't know how I got or what it means. Will you help me?"

Yes, of course, dear, you are so good too. Why are you

getting so formal? It's fine. Tell me how I can help you."

Bhavna responded.

I slowly raised my salwar to show her the scar on my left rib,

and her eyes dilated.

"How did you get that?"

"I don't know!" I was completely unaware.

3 : The Trump Card

I was waiting for the results of my body scan when Anik called.

Anik had called me in the night also, but I had missed his calls as my phone was in my room, and I had slept in Bhavna's room last night. I had seen his calls when I got ready, but I was rushing with Bhavna to her hospital.

The place was very crowded, so I messaged Anik and will talk later. Bhavna was a nurse at this hospital, and she looked worried when she came out.

"Rani, there is a problem, and I don't know how you do not know about it."

"I was equally tensed; what do you mean by a problem? Please tell me!" I pleaded.

"It's not a good place to talk; I want to discuss this with you in detail, so please wait until the evening. I will explain to you the reason behind your mark."

She gave me money and asked me to relax and go back home while she got busy attending to the patients.

I was clueless and thought of calling Anik.

"Where the hell are you? I was calling you frantically last night!" Anik blasted me.

"Yes, the phone was not near me, but listen to me."

"You listen to me; we have a trump card." Anik cut me in the middle.

"What do you mean by that?"

"Let's meet; I will tell you in person. Should I come over to your place?"

"Hmm, okay, I was out; reach my place in twenty minutes, is that fine?" I asked Anik.

"Sweetheart, I am at your place, but I will wait. Come fast!"

I was shocked to hear he was already at my place, and what was this sudden use of sweetheart? He was acting weird today. Anyway, I agreed and cut the phone.

What was happening to me? Except for me, everyone else had a clue; I had become a joke for myself and was lost!

I was frankly losing my sanity, but I tried to gather myself somehow.

"Taxi!!!"

When the taxi stopped at my place, Anik was waiting on his Royal Enfield in front of our hostel. He paid the taxi fare, held my hand, took me to my room, and closed the doors.

"Why are you looking so dull? I have some good news for you, and we have to go to Hyderabad!" Anik said this with excitement.

"What! Why Hyderabad?"

"Because I have made that Peon Shantu tell me everything!" Anik beamed.

"Oh, Wow, this is great news! Tell me everything, Anik!"

"Yes, I will, but first, we have to leave for Hyderabad. I have already booked the flight tickets, and we have to start by nine tonight."

"Hey, wait, you mean tonight? I have an important work tonight!" I remembered Bhavna was going to explain the scan report to me.

"What important work! What is more important than this, Rani? I have been trying to crack this case for you only, leaving the rest of the work to you!" Anik was getting angry.

"Okay! Yes, I know, but another thing came up last night, and I am trying to figure that out too!"

"What is that?"

I wasn't sure myself, and I didn't want to panic him too, so I thought of not telling him about the scar I had discovered on my left rib, for which Bhavna asked me to get a body scan done.

"Nothing serious; it was about a job!" I tried to divert the topic.

Anik stared at me as if he would kill me with his eyes alone.

"Okay, fine, yes, I am in; let me get ready then, and what about the story of Hyderabad? Why are we going there?"

"That's fine; I will tell you on the way! But this trump card,

Shantu, will help us solve your case; I am pretty confident!"

Anik said it with confidence.

4 : The Chance

A two-hour flight with a talkative seatmate, and before I knew it, we were ready to land. Thanks to Anik and the intriguing story he shared about the person we were meeting in Hyderabad, I didn't realize how quickly the flight time passed.

Fifteen years ago, India was still an unknown entity, not yet recognized as a booming economy to the world. The medical science field heavily relied on developed countries like North America, Europe, and the Middle East. However, during that time, a miraculous development was underway.

The advent of digital tools helped propel Indian technology in the medical field, creating new requirements and opportunities for those involved and opening doors to unprecedented revenue. Now, you might wonder why I'm discussing this. Well, there is a connection, and the circumstances I find myself in today, are connected to these advancements in medical science.

Let me take you back to Muskaan's story. She was an orphan having a strong desire to become a doctor, driven by her love for her late mother, Nikhat. Muskaan's father, Ali, had received a death sentence for her mother's murder, leaving her with no one to take care of her. As a result, she developed the mental strength to make decisions for herself.

Becoming a doctor meant gaining a reputation and earning enough money to uplift herself. Unfortunately, the government orphanage offered no opportunities for quality education. Nonetheless, Muskaan persevered, working hard to study and achieve good grades. Her dream was to gain admission to a reputable medical college, but destiny had something different for her.

Muskaan's warden, Alka, was a ruthless woman. She held a deep prejudice against her. It was due to Muskaan's father, Ali, since he got convicted of the murder of his wife. Alka despised Muskaan saying, "You have criminal blood!". Alka was narrow-minded and took pleasure in causing trouble, but Muskaan never retaliated.

One day, after Muskaan's tenth-grade results were out and she had cleared with distinction, Alka called her into her office. Muskaan, aware of her results, feared that Alka would not allow her to pursue further studies.

"Congratulations, Muskaan! You have cleared with distinction. It is a proud moment for our orphanage. I have more good news for you!" Alka said while swaying in her specially cushioned rolling chair.

"Thank you so much, Alka Ma'am! Please tell me!" Muskaan beamed.

"We have an offer to send you to Saudi Arabia for further studies. You are so brilliant that you have secured sponsorship for your desired medical career!"

Muskaan couldn't believe her ears. She was shocked that Alka, who had shown such disdain towards her, was helping her fulfill her dream of becoming a doctor. Her mother's dream was finally becoming a reality, so she couldn't resist the sponsorship and agreed to go to Saudi Arabia.

In the following days, the necessary formalities were all completed. A person arrived to accompany Muskaan. Little did she know then that her life would take a drastic turn.

Upon reaching Saudi Arabia, Muskaan quickly realized that Alka had sabotaged her future. She later discovered that Alka had received a decent ransom for selling her to a Saudi Sheikh. Muskaan found herself confined to a large room with several other girls. All of them were orphans sold from their respective countries, Malaysia, Bangladesh, Africa, and India. They were assigned various tasks in a hospital, serving as assistant nurses and working tirelessly from morning to night. The only time they were not under strict supervision was when they slept. Roll calls at every hour. They got treated like prisoners.

This life was even worse than the prison-like existence Muskaan had endured in the orphanage. Without her passport and no means of escape, she reluctantly accepted her fate. Moreover, one morning, her mother's last gift, a set of glass bangles, broke, symbolizing the shattering of her dreams.

Instead of crying, Muskaan got determined to become strong and resilient. Until then, her sole goal had been to become a doctor, but the current circumstances had altered her path. Legality or illegality no longer mattered to her; she had to find a way to create opportunities for herself using her training as a nurse.

Fortune, perhaps misfortune, provided her with opportunities to assist doctors during surgeries. Being a quick learner, she grasped the procedures with ease. In a matter of months, she became an expert, and her life took a turn.

Eventually, she encountered a doctor willing to make her a quack. She became an illegal doctor and started earning on her own.

After a few years of earning in Saudi Arabia, Muskaan planned to settle in India as she didn't want to return to Bangladesh. India was a budding market globally for affordable transplant surgeries. She established her clinic and settled in Hyderabad, gaining fame as a doctor renowned for performing transplants.

And now, she is connected to me. Muskaan is part of the illegal organ trafficking business. Bhavna called to inform me that my scan revealed that the lower lobe of my left lung was missing, explaining the scar on my left rib.

I was missing a lung because of Muskaan, the illegal doctor we were about to meet in Hyderabad.

5 : The Well

I was anxiously waiting!

I was outside the police station while Anik interrogated the fake doctor, Muskaan. Her screams and shouts claiming innocence reached my ears, but Anik persisted with questioning.

Earlier, Anik had introduced me to a constable named Bhanu Garu, who always smiled at me and asked if I needed anything. I declined his offer and occupied myself with my phone.

Just a few days ago, I was consumed by fear, unsure if I would ever uncover the truth about those three missing months of my life. A week later, currently, I knew enough about what had transpired.

I, owed my gratitude to Anik for helping me through this ordeal. I also realised he was an exceptionally sharp police officer, and fortunate to count him as a friend.

Yesterday, upon arriving in Hyderabad, we went to Muskaan's clinic. Anik instructed me to wear a mask to avoid getting recognized. A token system was there to meet her at her clinic, and we patiently awaited our turn.

Finally, when our turn came, we entered Muskaan's chamber. Despite my masked appearance, she somehow recognized me. I couldn't fathom how, but she immediately tried to flee from her seat. Anik swiftly apprehended her at gunpoint, ensuring she offered no resistance.

While I was lost, in my thoughts about the events, from the previous day, a sudden commotion erupted, grabbing my attention.

I looked around and witnessed cops rushing toward the entrance. Soon, an officer entered the premises, followed by the swarm of law enforcement personnel, all converging on the room Anik had entered.

Curiosity piqued, I stopped a passing constable and inquired, "What's happening? Who is he?"

The constable responded, "Rani Madam, you're with Anik Sir, Correct? He is the Commissioner. He has come to meet Anik Sir. I believe they have obtained significant leads."

Excitement surged within me upon hearing this news. Being a reporter, I was naturally intrigued to discover what was unfolding inside.

However, as I attempted to observe discreetly and went near the room Anik was in, the same constable caught me eavesdropping and firmly declared, "Rani Madam, please stay outside. It is highly confidential, and I've been given strict orders not to allow anyone in."

"But I'm a witness to the crime, and perhaps I could provide them with crucial information!" I tried to persuade him.

The constable appeared puzzled, knocking on the commissioner's door. After a few minutes, he emerged with a sorrowful expression and conveyed, "No, Madam, you cannot be permitted. I apologize for the inconvenience. Should I arrange some food for you?"

"No, it's alright. I'm not hungry. I'll wait outside," I replied, comprehending the gravity of the situation. Unless Anik emerged, I wouldn't glean any clues. Impatience was not an option, and waiting became my sole course of action.

Eventually, hunger gnawed at me, and I contemplated heading to the tea stall across the station.

I stepped out of the police station compound, preparing to cross the road, when a white Maruti van screeched to halt suddenly infront of me.

Masked men emerged, forcefully pulling me into the van. Before I could react or scream, they injected me with some drug, and everything faded into darkness.

When I opened my eyes again, it was dark all around. This place looked like a well, and a dim light coming from the roof. I felt like something or someone was watching me, and when I turned my eyes toward my left side, it was an uncanny visual.

Two glowing eyes were staring at me, and their uncanny presence signalled that I was in danger again!

6 : Heads or Tails

Whenever Magan was confused about his bet, he used to do a head or tail to check his chance, and surprisingly, it indicated his luck for the day very well. But today, the trick didn't work.

It was a slow start when he woke up; his head was still spinning due to the effect of last night's imported single malt, not due to quality, but because he had suddenly changed his taste from the local whisky to a branded one.

He was just wondering how to get rid of this headache when the phone on his side table started ringing. He picked it up; it was Shantu, the peon from the pathology centre.

"Yes, Shantu, why are you calling so early?"

"Early, what early? It's already noon, and I have been trying to reach you since morning. Where were you?" Shantu was breathless.

Magan looked at the table clock; his eyes barely opened. Oh, yes, it's noon, so what happened? Why are you trying to call me?"

"They took me, inquired a lot, and even beat me like hell, so I had to tell them about you and Doctor Madam!" Shantu was sobbing and had a hoarse voice.

"Who are they, and what did you tell them? Stop crying; tell me what happened." Magan screamed at Shantu; he was fully awake now.

"Police, who else? They have found our racket, Magan Sir! We are doomed!" Shantu cut the phone off.

Magan's mind just exploded; everything was flashing in front of him: the kidnappings, the unsuccessful operation, the dead body disposal, and then the recent deal of six million.

Last night he got advance money for the assignments. Two kidney and two lung transplant patients were ready, and he had to give the money to Siraj for the preparation. The girls were already kidnapped and secured for the operation, and the blood tests were completed and checked for matches. The Doctor will come in the next week. So everything is as per plan. Then how come this sudden Police business? Even if the person who supported them from the local administration was well-bribed, why were the Cops after him? Who inquired about Shantu, and why did he say being beaten up? But something struck him then.

"No, this can't be true; how could I trust this idiot Shantu? If he was caught already by the Cops, how did he get released to call me? Oh No! It's a trap; he must have called to know where I am. I have to run."

In the meantime, at the Police Station, based on Shantu's call, Shaheed had tracked Magan's location. Anik's colleague was conducting his investigation while Anik was visiting the Doctor. Shaheed was doing a background check on Magan and found he was a bodyguard turned criminal. Sometime back, he had been caught on organ trafficking grounds but released by the court due to a lack of solid evidence.

Aware of Magan's dangerous background, Shaheed immediately alarmed the cops at his location. His hideout was known now, and he told the local inspector to arrest him.

Magan tossed a coin, hoping if heads he might get saved somehow, and he got heads.

"Yes, I still have a chance to run away from the police."

He got up and took some clothes and the bag with four million rupees in cash. But then there was a knock at his door.

Magan looked from the window and saw a tall man near his door.

"Oh my God, police!" He quickly opened the back door and was about to jump when the front door opened, and the police officer shot a bullet in his leg.

"Magan, You are arrested for an illegal organ trafficking racket." The inspector said this while pointing his pistol at him.

7 : Colours of Love

Forty-five years ago, in a small county north of Prague, lived a happy couple named Shirla and Yuzuf. They had fled during the war and resided with a new identity now.

On a cold December day, after enduring eighteen hours of labor pain, Shirla gave birth to a beautiful boy. The doctor, who was their neighbour and regarded Shirla as a younger sister, had saved her and arranged her marriage to Yuzuf after she lost her parents and property during the insurgency. Later, he also escaped with them to Prague.

The couple named their son Mifrah, as he had brought immense happiness into their lives. Yuzuf, an artist by profession, struggled to find stable employment. He eventually secured a waiter job in a nearby restaurant. Shirla, on the other hand, possessed computer skills and managed to secure a desk clerk job in a bank through the doctor's reference.

Many years later, during dinner one night, there was a sudden knock on the door. Yuzuf went to answer it, only to be shot by a tall man wearing dark glasses who barged into their house. The intruder began searching through the drawers while Shirla, having heard the gunshot, was about to scream when a hand covered her face from behind and pulled her into Mifrah's room.

Mifrah, a genius, intelligent child for his age, sensed the danger and was determined to protect his mother. As soon as the tall man entered his room, Mifrah's latent superpower took over, and he swiftly plunged a knife into the intruder's leg. When the man fell, Mifrah decisively slit his throat.

Shirla was shocked to witness the ferociousness of her fifteen-year-old son. She couldn't believe he was her child and remained calm, holding his hand and embracing him.

Filled with fear that they would end up in jail if anyone found out about the incident, Shirla cleaned up the mess and instructed Mifrah not to disclose anything to anyone. Yuzuf was gone, and now Mifrah was all she had.

Mifrah smiled at his mother, but deep inside, he got ecstatic thrill at the sight of the blood flowing from the intruder's body. Mifrah had previously stolen something valuable, blood diamonds worth fifty million dollars, from the tall man while he was dining at the restaurant where Yuzuf worked as a waiter. That's why Mifrah was already aware of the man's presence.

In the following months, Mifrah found ways to make more money and began engaging in betting. With his computer skills, he delved into hacking, getting caught a couple of times but escaping punishment due to his influential doctor uncle's connections. Eventually, he established an unbeatable international business that involved organ trafficking to exploit desperate patients who were willing to undergo illegal transplantation due to the lengthy and costly legal processes.

Over the next few years, using his doctor uncle's fake ID, Mifrah hacked into the databases of major international hospitals. He compiled a database of patients seeking organ transplants from countries such as the Middle East, Europe, Germany, Russia, and many others.

That's where I, a nurse aspiring to become a doctor, came into the picture. Mifrah promoted me to the role of a quack doctor.

Muskaan had endured enough torture from Anik, forcing her to reveal this terrifying truth. She was Mifrah's girlfriend and had recently lost their son, who had gone missing.

Anik realized the magnitude of the racket and understood that Muskaan was one of the links in this chain. However, he also realized he couldn't apprehend Mifrah without the assistance of higher authorities. The case exceeded his pay grade. Consequently, Anik promptly contacted his senior in Kolkata, who later connected him with the Commissioner. It led to the meeting between Anik and the Hyderabad Commissioner. Unknown to them, Rani, was kidnapped again, and her life was in imminent danger.

Will Anik be able to save Rani?

8 : Deja Vu

When I opened my eyes again, it was dark all around. This place looked like a well, and a dim light coming from the roof.

I felt like something or someone was watching me, and when I turned my eyes toward my left side, it was an uncanny visual.

Two glowing eyes were staring at me, and their uncanny presence signalled that I was in danger again!

~~~~~~~

I realised being greeted by the awful stench of raw meat that permeated the air around me, revealing the ominous presence of a creature with glowing green eyes lurking in the shadows.
~~~~~~~

I couldn't scream, only to discover that I was gagged and unable to make a sound. My hands were tightly bound behind the chair, leaving me helpless and vulnerable. Oh no, I got kidnapped again.

The realisation struck me like a bolt of lightning—I had fallen into the clutches of a different kind of danger. No longer was I with my trusted friend Anik. Instead, I was again in the clutch of a group of unknown kidnappers who had prepared well for my arrival.

I was panicking now as I adjusted to this dimly lit place.

Fear gripped my heart, but this time I wasn't going to succumb to despair.

My mind was racing, reflecting on the choices that had led me to this terrifying moment, regretting not informing anyone of my plans to leave the police station. If only I had requested the assistance of the hawaldar or ensured someone knew my whereabouts, I might have avoided this dire predicament. I am sure those criminals were keeping a watch on us when we took the doctor to the police station. That is how they immediately captured me when I came out. But it was too late for regrets now; I had to focus on finding a way out.

While surveying my surroundings, I tried to find any possible means of escape. The faint light revealed a few scattered crates in the corners. The walls were grimy, and the air felt heavy with a foreboding presence. It became clear that I was in an old, abandoned dungeon—a perfect hideout for goons.

Though my heart raced with fear, my determination burned brighter than ever. I was unprepared, but I knew that my survival depended on my ability to outsmart my Kidnappers. With some great effort, I wriggled and twisted my body, inching the chair closer to an old wooden crate near my reach. With all my strength, I moved until I knocked that crate over, causing a loud crash that reverberated through that well.

I hoped that the noise wasn't loud to attract attention, but then the creature roared and almost came near my face, but then stopped!

I could smell its awful breath, and was scared to the core; it was a deadly hour. I also realised it might be a panther or leopard, but it was chained, hence, couldn't reach me. Thank God; otherwise, I would have been dead meat.

My ears caught the sound of hurried footsteps approaching the well. Moments later, a door burst open at one side of the well, revealing a group of armed men who stared at me.

One of these men said, "So, Rani madam, are you awake now?"

As my eyes, were locked with the armed men, a shiver of apprehension ran down my spine. Their words confirmed my suspicions. They knew my name, and it was evident that this was not a random kidnapping. They had specifically targeted me.

Rani madam? The familiarity with which the man addressed my name indicated they had been monitoring me, observing my every move. Questions were swirling in my mind, searching for answers. Were they the same men who had kidnapped me earlier or a different set of goons?

Suppressing my fear, I gathered my courage and forced myself to stay composed.

With a steady voice, I asked, "Who are you? What do you want from me?"

The man who had spoken earlier sneered, a chilling smile spread across his face.

"We are the ones who deal in valuable commodities, Rani madam. And you, my Madam, are the most precious commodity, we have ever laid, our eyes on."

9 : Life or Death

My heart sank as I realized the true nature of their intentions. They were not just kidnappers seeking ransom or revenge; they were organ traffickers. Perhaps they were the same ones I had encountered before, though I was unconscious then, and now, I am fully awake. My worst fears were becoming a reality once again.

As I struggled against my restraints, a glimmer of hope flickered in my mind. If these men saw me as a valuable commodity, I could use that to my advantage. I needed to find a way to outsmart them, buy myself some time, and create an opportunity for escape.

Drawing upon my inner strength, I locked eyes with the man who seemed to be their leader. "If you're looking for a valuable commodity, you should know that I can offer you something even more precious than organs," I said with a voice filled with determination.

Intrigued, the man leaned in, his curiosity piqued. "Oh, you know your organs are valuable. What else do you have that is more precious?" he asked.

"My knowledge!" I replied.

My mind raced for a plan. "I have insights into police operations about a significant development regarding your operations. Spare my life, and I will help you win over cops. Think about the consequences if your entire network is busted. Otherwise, all of you will be in prison for the rest of your life!"

The men exchanged glances, contemplating my proposition. Fear was evident in their eyes, and they were willing to entertain the idea. But I still had to convince them that my knowledge was valuable—the only ticket to survival.

Time was at a standstill as they deliberated. The seconds felt like an eternity, hanging between life and death. I prayed that my words had sparked their interest enough to spare me, even if only temporarily.

Finally, the leader nodded, a wicked grin stretching across his face. "Very well, Rani madam. We shall see if you're as valuable as you claim. But before that, I will call someone to confirm. However, one wrong move, and you will die!"

My heart skipped a beat, a mix of relief and trepidation flooding in. I had bought myself some time, but the stakes were higher than ever. I had to stay one step ahead, navigate the treacherous path before me, and ultimately find a way to turn the tables on these kidnappers.

With my life hanging in the balance, my long, sad journey had taken yet another dark turn, thrusting me into a dangerous dance of life or death.

The carnivore looked at me with its fierce green eyes, and let out a low growl, restrained by the chains that prevented it from reaching me. It paced back and forth, agitated by the intrusion of the men into its territory. Sensing an opportunity amidst the confusion, I realized the dangerous creature could turn the tide in my favour.

As the armed men cautiously approached me while their leader went to make a call, their focus solely on me, I mustered the courage to act. In a split-second decision, I quickly moved toward the chained carnivore, jumping from my position and using my bound hands to provoke it into action.

It was a leopard; I could see the round spots in the dim light.

The leopard sensing my movement within its grasp, roared louder this time, terrifying the men. In an unexpected turn of events, the leopard pounced on one of the men, scratching his face. Miraculously, its chain broke, and with a newfound sense of achievement, the powerful and heavy leopard leaped into action, attacking the remaining men.

The room erupted into chaos as the wild predator unleashed its fury upon the goons, clawing and biting with a ferocity that sent them scattering in fear. Their guns fell to the ground, forgotten, in the face of the untamed force which dominated this place now.

I had my chance to live, or was it to die?

10 : The Chase

As chaos erupted within the room, the men were frantically trying to defend themselves against the unleashed fury of the hungry carnivore.

My mind raced with a newfound realisation. Calling me Rani Madam by the leader had triggered a connection within my memory—the same way the hawaldar at the police station had addressed me.

My thoughts raced back to my encounter with the hawaldar and the peculiar familiarity he had shown towards me as if that was only because of Anik, or did he already know me? Could he be somehow connected to these organ traffickers? Was he involved in their nefarious operation?

Determined to uncover the truth, I focused on freeing my hands first. I wiggled and twisted, using every ounce of my strength to loosen the ropes that held me captive. The adrenaline coursing through my veins fuelled my determination to escape with each passing second.

I eventually untied my hands as the spotted animal continued its relentless assault. I had no time to waste; quickly scrambling to my feet, I even bruised myself during the ordeal. But my priority was to run away from these dangerous men as soon as possible; hence, ignoring these wounds, I tried to stand and moved towards the exit.

Barefoot and disoriented, I carefully navigated the chaotic scene, sidestepping the struggling men and watching the Leopard's movements. The unleashed rage of the predator provided a much-needed diversion, buying me precious moments to attempt my escape.

I inched my way toward the exit, my heart throbbing as I took each cautious step. Every sound and every movement heightened my senses, reminding me of the imminent danger I was in. Yet determination and desperation fuelled my every move.

Just as I reached the threshold of freedom, a voice from behind startled me.

"Leaving so soon, Rani Madam? I am surprised you excited my pet Leopard to eat my men only! That was a smart move!"

I froze, my heart sinking, as I turned to face the leader of those goons. A malicious smile passed on his face. He had managed to evade the Leopard's wrath because it was his pet, but being hungry, when it got free, it pounded on the others. It was clear that my attempt to free the Leopard was a blessing in disguise, but my escape had not gone unnoticed.

Without wasting another moment, I ran towards the exit, my bare feet hitting the cold ground full of human bones. My lungs burned with each gasping breath, but I refused to let exhaustion deter me. I had come too far to surrender now.

I could sense that the leader was giving chase, his footsteps thundering behind me. I zigzagged through the dark, unfamiliar terrain, desperately seeking refuge and a chance to survive.

As I darted through the night, a glimmer of hope emerged in the distance—a small, dilapidated building partially hidden within a thicket of trees. It seemed like my only chance at evading capture. Summoning the last traces of my strength, I pushed myself forward, reaching the shelter just as the leader closed in.

With bated breath, I slipped through the broken doorway, my heart pounding heavily. The building offered a temporary respite—momentary salvation from the relentless pursuit. I pressed myself against a wall. My body trembled with exhaustion and fear as I desperately sought a plan for what lay ahead.

In the darkness of the abandoned building, I knew my journey was far from over. Resolute to save my life and ensure my safety first, I had evaded the immediate threat. Though the mysteries surrounding my kidnapping and the potential involvement of the hawaldar still loomed large, I was determined to uncover the truth now.

Could I survive this situation on my own? I steeled myself for the challenges ahead of me.

11 : A Godly Wish

It was an old, dilapidated place. Cobwebs greeted my eyes in every corner. It resembled a haunted mansion, but I had no other choice. In that moment of fear, meeting a ghost seemed preferable to encountering that leader.

The timid version of myself, afraid of the supernatural, had transformed into a brave individual.

However, I had brought this situation upon myself. If I hadn't slipped out of the station unnoticed, perhaps I wouldn't have faced my second kidnapping. Did destiny intend for me to confront the dangers of my past and emerge stronger by facing them? Dwelling on the past served no purpose now.

As my mind raced, desperately desiring a glimmer of hope, thoughts of Anik crossed my mind. Could he be the ray of light I needed in this dire situation? With a flicker of faith, I silently prayed. I hoped that Anik would come to my aid. I didn't know how I still held onto the hope that he could find me. I had witnessed his unwavering courage and resourcefulness before, and I prayed that he would sense my distress and find a way to help me.

Amid my desperate plea, I caught a faint rustling sound, diverting my attention. Had the leader somehow entered the building? Did I have to run from this place now? I turned towards the noise, my heart racing with anticipation. Would the leader find me again?

Footsteps approached, growing closer. In that darkness and the abandoned place, I held my breath. I hoped to remain unnoticed, but the footsteps were still approaching me.

To my astonishment, a familiar face emerged from the shadows. Relief flooded over me, washing away my fear.

Anik stepped forward, his face etched with concern. "Rani, I had a feeling something was wrong. I've been searching for you!" Anik's voice conveyed a mix of happiness and concern.

Relief surged through me as I gazed into Anik's eyes. I could hardly believe he had found me in this remote and treacherous location. It felt as if my wish got granted. I was fortunate. Thank you, God, for being there! I knew I could rely on Anik to guide me through this darkness.

"I'm so glad you're here, but how did you find me?" I whispered, my voice trembling with gratitude and surprise.

"That's a story. When I came out, you were nowhere to be found, and no one knew where you were. I couldn't reach you on your phone. I was worried!" Anik sounded tense.

"I had a hunch that maybe these traffickers had captured you since I had apprehended their doctor. I checked all the CCTV footage and discovered you got kidnapped from the police station's main gate. I managed to get the car's license plate details. We were tracing the car, and that's when I ended up near this place and saw you running! Did they torture you?"

"These are dangerous criminals, organ traffickers. And there's something suspicious about the constable at the police station. I believe he's involved in organ trafficking too, Anik."

Anik's eyes widened with a mixture of concern and conviction. "We'll get to the bottom of this, Rani. But first, we need to get you to safety. My men are already here. If the constable is connected, these criminals must have fled by now. Your suspicion about him makes sense now. He intended to mislead me into thinking you had returned to the hotel, wasting our time so that these individuals could hide you beyond our reach!"

"Together, we need to devise a plan to elude the remaining threats and gather the evidence to expose all the criminals and their connections. The main culprits are already in our custody, that includes the kidnapper Magan, the doctor Muskaan, and now Mifrah, their kingpin. There are a few more accomplices we need to catch. So, even if some police officers are involved, we will uncover those moles too."

I felt relieved hearing Anik's words. Once again grateful to have him as my true friend. At that moment, I couldn't have asked for anything more!

12 : Justice

In Anik's company, I had a fighting chance to unravel the truth and end the heinous operation that had plagued my life. We moved swiftly and stealthily through the shadows with caution. Anik's expertise in evading capture and knowledge of the criminal underworld proved invaluable as we made our way to a safe location.

The police had already surrounded the abandoned well and successfully captured the leopard and a few of the goons, who were still alive. However, the leader had managed to escape, and Anik now had strong suspicions about Hawaldar's involvement.

As the realization dawned on me that the leopard was the leader's pet, a chilling truth unfolded.

The leader had orchestrated the brutal attack at the hostel, using the leopard as a diversion to execute his sinister plan of kidnapping new victims; while attention was elsewhere. The innocent children at the hostel got caught in the crossfire, their lives endangered while chaos ensued. Shock and fear were the perfect weapons in the leader's twisted strategy to kidnap without suspicion.

The gravity of the situation weighed heavily on me as I realized we had to act swiftly to end this reign of terror. When I shared this newfound knowledge with Anik, he was equally stunned by the revelation. Anik's mission to rescue me had transformed into something considerably greater. We had to urgently race against time to prevent more innocent lives from falling into the clutches of these dangerous criminals.

Together, we devised a plan to expose Mifrah and his depraved operation. Anik leveraged the knowledge of Quack Doctor Muskaan and Kidnapper Magan to extract more details about their connections, processes, and any officer involvement.

In pursuit of justice, we encountered danger at every turn. Mifrah's henchmen followed us for a few days, but we narrowly escaped traps set by these criminals because Magan had become our well-wisher, providing us with information. Through Magan, we came to know about Adhikari.

Though Adhikari and Mifrah tried to kill Magan more than once, Anik saved his life. Hence, Magan had become loyal to us.

With Muskaan's help over a month, we identified all the patient criteria and found the hospitals they operated from. We discreetly gathered information that delved deeper into Mifrah and Adhikari's connections and activities. This investigation took us through a labyrinth of secret operations and corrupt individuals, with each step pushing us closer to the heart of the criminal empire.

Over the coming days, Anik and I meticulously pieced together their network puzzle. We uncovered a group of corrupted hospital staff, doctors, and senior officers that extended far beyond what we had initially imagined.

With Magan's help, I also uncovered how they took assistance from Bhavna in procuring a list of candidates who met the blood test requirements. Based on this evidence, we gathered enough proof against Mifrah and his collaborators, connecting all the dots.

When we brought the evidence to light, exposing the truth of organ trafficking to the authorities, the revelation sent shockwaves through the administration. It ignited a call for change and demanded swift action against those involved. The leader of Indian operations, Adhikari, the one I had encountered, along with his accomplices Siraj and others, were apprehended, and the entire organ trafficking network, including Mifrah's accomplices, was arrested.

In the end, we were able to expose and dismantle this nefarious network, not only in India but also in major countries around the world. These dangerous criminals got punished under the laws of their respective countries with the joint help of the Central Administration, the Hyderabad and Kolkata Commissioners, and International Police support. The truth behind the involvement of the hawaldar and some other senior cops at the police station got also revealed, uncovering a web of corruption that reached high levels of administration.

Though our journey was fraught with danger and close calls, our bond grew stronger with every obstacle we overcame. I drew strength from Anik's unwavering support, and he drew strength from my courage in the pursuit of truth. In his office, everybody started acknowledging our partnership as a formidable force against the darkness, and we were known as 'The Vigilantes' couple.

Goodness Always Wins

If you still remember Shantanu, Gagandeep's math teacher, who adopted an orphan on the day of the leopard attack and wondered what happened to him? Here is an update.

He discovered that the orphan he adopted was the son of a criminal doctor named Muskaan. The eleven-year-old boy, Vihaan, loved his Mom Muskaan, and enjoyed spending time with her. However, he became curious about his father's whereabouts and questioned Muskaan repeatedly. She would deflect his questions, stating that his father lived abroad. However, Vihaan's persistence led Muskaan to promise to introduce him to his father soon.

During the summer vacation, Muskaan took Vihaan to Araku Valley, where they stayed in a resort with a picturesque view.

Vihaan was excited about meeting his father, and Muskaan introduced him to a man named Mifrah.

Mifrah was overjoyed to meet Vihaan and showered him with gifts. Spending time with his father was a dream come true for Vihaan, but fate had other plans.

One night while engrossed with his new toys, Vihaan noticed that both Muskaan and Mifrah were absent. Curiosity got the better of him and made him go out to search for them.

As he passed by some resort cottages, he overheard a familiar voice coming from one of them. Intrigued, Vihaan approached that cottage and peered through the window. He saw Muskaan, Mifrah, and another man engaged in a discussion inside that place.

Vihaan contemplated knocking on the door but hesitated when he overheard the word 'kidnap' in their conversation.

Driven by curiosity, he strained his ears to listen to their discussion. He was shocked by what he discovered.

"You need to be more careful with these kidnaps. Last time two out of four survived the organ operation. You cannot kidnap anaemic people; better you do some background checks before kidnapping them. We don't want to get on the Police wanted list for murderers. Do you understand me?" Muskaan was scolding the man with the beard.

It became evident to Vihaan that his mother was involved in criminal activities. He felt a mixture of shock and fear but resolved to uncover the truth. Quietly, he returned to his room without raising any suspicions.

That night, when Muskaan and Mifrah returned, they had dinner together as if nothing had happened. Vihaan acted normal, concealing the unsettling question that plagued his mind: Who was that bearded man?

Listening to his mother and Mifrah converse, Vihaan realized they were still discussing organ trafficking using coded language.

Being a smart kid, he managed to glimpse Muskaan's phone dial list while they were preoccupied. 'Adhikari' was the first entry on the list.

The next day, Vihaan observed the bearded man closely and was surprised to discover that he accompanied a young boy, Gagandeep. Vihaan tried to befriend Gagandeep, but Adhikari prevented them from getting too close. Soon after this, Adhikari left the resort. Despite the obstructions, Vihaan got Gagandeep's contact number before Adhikari's departure.

The next day while leaving the resort, Vihaan decided to run away once he reached home. Mifrah hugged him, but Vihaan felt no emotional connection. Just a few days earlier, he was excited to meet his father. But now he felt repulsed by the truth that his father was a criminal. His hands which hugged him and gifted him toys had killed someone.

Once they reached Hyderabad, Vihaan wasted no time and escaped from his mother's house. He believed it was better to be an orphan than the son of a criminal.

Vihaan messaged Gagandeep, informing him that his father was a wanted criminal. He wandered on the streets for a few days before he encountered Shantanu.

Initially, Vihaan kept his family background a secret. But later, due to Meena's influence (Shantanu's wife) and the love he received from Shantanu, he decided to confess the truth to them. Vihaan was playing the mouth organ when Rani asked him about the place and date in the streets of Chinatown. He had beautiful turquoise eyes.

Meanwhile, Rani and Anik tirelessly worked to dismantle the empire of darkness involved in human trafficking. With the support of the Commissioner, they saved numerous lives and ensured the victims' rehabilitation and protection.

Throughout their journey, Rani and Anik's bond grew stronger as they shared their experiences, eventually falling in love.

Although they carried physical and emotional scars from the horrors they witnessed, they found solace in knowing their courage and perseverance had made a difference. They served, as an inspiration to others, proving that even in the darkest times, hope for a better tomorrow exists.

Currently, Rani has started her reporting channel on YouTube, attracting millions of followers.

Anik is promoted to Senior Inspector, bringing pride to his family. He is no longer recognized solely for his father's reputation but for his bravery and courage.

Together, Rani and Anik continue to fight against human trafficking. They are on a mission to build stronger laws and support systems, raising awareness to prevent others from suffering the same fate.

They have exchanged marriage vows and also vows to remain vigilant, understanding that the world will always need superheroes willing to confront the darkness and offer hope to those trapped within its grasp.

~ ~ ~ ~xXx~ ~ ~ ~

A Thank You Note

to make improvements in future.

Thank you so much!

Siddharth Sen

PLEASE FILL THIS SURVEY LINK TO TELL ABOUT YOUR
FEEDBACK AND GET EXCITING OFFERS FROM AUTHOR

About the Author

*EMERGING FROM A MODEST BACKGROUND, **AUTHOR SIDDHARTH SEN'S** ROOTS TRACE BACK TO THE PICTURESQUE LANDSCAPES OF A QUAINT VALLEY TOWN DEHRADUN, UTTARAKHAND, INDIA WHERE AUTHOR RUSKIN BOND LIVES.*

AT THE AGE OF 6, SIDDHARTH WAS ALREADY WRITING POEMS FILLED WITH LOVE FOR NATURE.

*WINNER OF THE SUPER WRITER JUDGES CHOICE AWARD AND IAA VOICE AWARD, SIDDHARTH'S PUBLISHED WORKS INCLUDE BESTSELLERS LIKE **"ADVENTURES OF SAMI"**, **"THE GIRL IN THE WELL"**, **"MY BEST FRIEND"** SERIES, **"MY LIFE IN POEMS"** AN ACCLAIMED POET AMONG BLOOMING POETS OF INDIA. HE HAS WRITTEN MANY MORE FICTION AND NON FICTION STORIES IN WRITING PLATFORMS. APART FROM HIS BOOKS, HE IS A CLARITY COACH, NATURE LOVER, TRAVELLER AND FOUNDER OF SID's ACHIEVER CLUB. HIS BOOKS ARE AVAILABLE ON AMAZON, NOTION, BARNES & NOBLES, KOBO AND MANY OTHER PLATFORMS ALL OVER THE WORLD.*

SCAN TO KNOW MORE ABOUT SIDDHARTH AND TO CONNECT @